16.99

EVANSTON PUBLIC LIBRARY

3 1192 01125 8959

WITHDRAWN

x811 Grime.N

Grimes, Nikki.

Stepping out with
 Grandma Mac /

DATE DUE

MAY 1 7 2001	
MAR 1 7 2004	
FEB 2 8 2005	
FEB 1 4 2008	

DEMCO, INC. 38-2931

W9-BPN-380

Stepping Out with Grandma Mac

Text copyright © 2001 by Nikki Grimes

Illustrations copyright © 2001 by Angelo

All rights reserved. No part of this book may be reproduced
or transmitted in any form or by any means, electronic or
mechanical, including photocopying, recording, or by any
information storage or retrieval system, without permission
in writing from the Publisher.

Orchard Books

An Imprint of Scholastic Inc.

95 Madison Avenue

New York, NY 10016

Manufactured in the United States of America

Printed and bound by Worzalla Publishing Co.

Book design by Mina Greenstein

The text of this book is set in 12 point Horley Old Style.

The illustrations are pencil.

10 9 8 7 6 5 4 3 2 1

Library of Congress Cataloging-in-Publication Data
Grimes, Nikki.
Stepping out with Grandma Mac / by Nikki Grimes ;
illustrated by Angelo.
p. cm.
Summary: Poems celebrate the special relationship between a feisty
grandmother and her equally spunky granddaughter.
ISBN 0-531-30320-9 (tr. : alk. paper)
1. Grandmothers—Juvenile poetry. 2. Children's poetry, American.
[1. Grandmothers—Poetry. 2. Afro-Americans—Poetry.
3. American poetry.] I. Angelo, date, ill. II. Title.
PS3557.R489982 S74 2001
811'.54—dc21 00-39979

For BERNICE,
who knows that some of us
learn love late
—N.G.

For MELVIN,
you are my pride
—A.

Contents

Grandma Mac

Most of my friends
Have at least one
Grandparent to spare,
And some have four
Or six or eight
Who debate
Which of them
Gets to borrow
The grandkid next.
As for me,
I've only got
One grandparent
Still living.
Then again
With Grandma Mac
I've pretty much got
My hands full.

First Impressions

At three I missed
The grandma in my mind,
The one who'd bounce me
On her knee, and read
Jack and the Beanstalk
While I flipped the pages.
The grandma who'd
Bake oatmeal cookies,
Take me to the zoo,
And spoil me with
Too much ice cream.
Of course,
Grandma lived miles away
Back then.

Now I'm ten
And too big to sit on
Anybody's knee.
Besides, the only bounce
My grandma has
Is in her high-heeled step
When she strides
Down the street, gathering
Men's glances.

She bakes, but only pies
At Christmas,
Hates the zoo,
And refuses to stuff me
With sweets.
Still, she's more adventurous
Than most grandmas
I know. And she never
Makes me guess
What's on her mind
Which is fine by me.
As for baking
Oatmeal cookies
And the rest,
Let's just say
Grandma Mac
Is a late bloomer.

Neat Freak

My room
Is a jigsaw puzzle
Of clothes and books
And dust-bunnies with
Babies of their own,
Which is why I lock
My bedroom door
When Grandma Mac
Comes around.
She can't abide
Dirt or clutter.
Dust leaves its
Calling card
At her front door,
Afraid to enter.
Her floors are raw
From scrubbing.
Her trash basket
Is hungry for scraps.

Even her kitchen sink
Sometimes wishes
It could keep a stack
Of dirty dishes
Overnight.
There's little chance
Of that, though,
'Cause Grandma Mac
Is a neat freak
And proud of it.

Sharp Tongue · · · · · · · · · · · · · · ·

It's not my fault
Grandma's kitchen floor
Is shiny as ice.
One afternoon
Alone for a minute
I give in to temptation,
Skate from stove to cabinet.
"Stop that!"
Says Grandma Mac.
"This is no place to play!"
I sulk my way
Into the living room,
Settle in a sofa chair,
Lift a doily resting there,
And poke my fingers
Through it.
"Put that back!"
Grandma snaps.
"Leave things
Where they belong!"

And so the day
Grinds on:
Don't sit there!
Don't touch that!
Don't run! Don't yell!
(*Don't breathe!*
I mutter to myself.)
"You shouldn't
Let her get to you,"
Mom says,
On hearing
My complaint.
"Your grandma
Is all bark."
"Oh, yeah?" I say.
"Then how come
There are teeth marks
In my heart?"

Grandma's Perfume Bottle

Here she comes
Spritzing me with cologne
Five seconds after
I hit the door.
She's armed and dangerous
With a dainty, cut-glass
Perfume bottle that
Catches the morning light
And flings it against the wall
Like pieces
Of shattered rainbow.
How she can afford such things
I'll never know.
But she says
Being poor is no excuse
For lacking such
Feminine essentials
As *eau de toilette.*

"Hold still. I'm not done yet,"
She tells me, dabbing
A little scent behind my ears,
And it doesn't much matter
That I'm wearing blue jeans
And a baseball cap
Because, she says,
"A real lady
Should always
Stink pretty."

Grandma's Table

Setting Grandma's table
Takes a while.
She's fussy about
Which dish goes where.
A knife, fork, and plate
(Plus food)
Is all I need,
Yet Grandma's bent on
Giving me The Drill.
She lays the silver out
For me to name:
Soup spoon, salad fork,
Smooth-as-butter knife,
Ladle, soup tureen,
(We've moved on to the dishes)
Dessert plate, salad bowl,
(We aren't having either!)
Juice glass, water glass,

Please-pass-me
The salt & pepper caddy.
I ask her why I need
To know what's what
And get the usual "Because."
I groan so loud
I'm sure the neighbors hear.
As for Grandma
She laughs and says,
"Someday
You'll thank me, dear."

Field Trip

Grandma drags me to
The Garment District
And school is in
The minute the bus
Spits us out
On the sidewalk.
"This way," she says,
Marching me into
One factory outlet
After another,
Stopping just long enough
To study a skirt hem
Or turn a jacket
Inside out
And lecture me
On its pedigree
With plans
To quiz me later.
(Which cloth was suede?
Which one imitation?)

"We're poor
And can't afford
The cheap stuff," she says.
"Our clothes
Have got to last."
So I suppose
We'll be taking
These field trips
Until I know my silk,
Tweed, wool gabardine,
And can spot
A well-sewn seam
At a glance.
It may be boring,
But if I pout
Or bat my lashes
A time or two,
I usually go home
Wearing something new.

~ 13

China Cabinet

The china cabinet
Bulges with temptation.
Sometimes I reach in,
Trace each goblet lip
With a greedy fingertip,
Measure Great-grandma's
Gold-rimmed platter
With the fan of my hand,
And caress the candy dish
That shimmers like
Polished sunset.
Grandma's quick rap
On my knuckles is never
Enough to make me
Sorry for my crime.
Besides, she uses these
Treasures all the time.
"Life is for living,
Not for show," she says.

"And I plan on enjoying
All I own before I go."
Seems smart to me
Though I need practice.
So today I remove
The candy dish,
Set it on the coffee table,
And peek at Grandma Mac
For approval.
She grunts, leaves the room,
And returns with
A bag of chocolate kisses
And a wink.

Grandma's Child

As far as I'm concerned
The only person
In this world I'm like
Is *me*. My mom
Says otherwise.
She calls me
Grandma's child.
"For starters," she says,
"In stubbornness,
The two of you are twins."
I shrug her comment off.
After all, she's *Mom*,
So how could she be right?
Grandma Mac and I
Both speak our minds,
It's true,
And maybe we both
Love corn pudding
With a burnt crust,
Hate imitation anything,
And believe royal blue
Is, by far, the best
Color in the rainbow.
Okay, so maybe Mom is right.
That doesn't mean
I have to tell her.

Window-Shopping

Grandma shops
For groceries.
She doesn't need
My expertise.
And yet I tag along.
We pass a jeweler's
On the way.
I slow to paw
The store window
And eye a bracelet
Thick with charms.
"Come on,"
Says Grandma,
Yanking me away.
"No window-shopping today."

The next week
Grandma breaks her rule
And bakes a pie
Though it's not Christmas.

She places a tiny
Gift beside it.
"Well, go on! Open it,"
She says,
Gruff as ever.
I tear into the box,
Find a familiar
Golden bracelet
Noisy with charms,
Gleaming like the light
In Grandma's eyes.

Fences

When I visit Grandma Mac
She usually snaps at me
To wipe my feet
On the welcome mat
So I don't dirty her rug.
There are no hugs,
No "Come here, sugar."
Just "Well, are you
Coming in or not?"
Her cold words
Used to make me shiver
Though never enough
To chase me away.
Then, after a while,
I'd notice how a light
Switches on in her eyes
Every time she sees me.

And I'd catch her
Sneaking money inside
My purse or pocket
So I could find it later
Like buried treasure.
And, more than once,
I saw her eyes
Bathe me with pride.
So I figure
Grandma's chilly words
Aren't brick walls
Made to keep me out.
They're more like picket fences
With gaps wide enough
For me to squeeze through—
All I have to do
Is try.

My math book snarls at me
While Grandma's happy fingers
Skip through her thesaurus
Jotting down a few new words
Along the way.
I shake my head thinking
She ought to be
The one in school.
It's clear which of us
likes study better.

Grandma says it's because
She slid through the Depression
On elbow grease. She paced
The Harlem streets each dawn
With other women who
Waited for the rich to arrive
In their shiny chariots, offering
A day's pay to have
Their silver spoons
Polished,
Their parquet floors
Hand-waxed,
Their porcelain toilets
Scrubbed squeaky clean.

"You should've seen
Those houses," Grandma says.
"Even the chandeliers tinkled
With the sound of money.
But, honey, all I wanted was a job."
If they chose her, that night
Her soup bones would be
Wearing a little meat.

So when I gripe about homework,
Grandma reminds me
How earning a G.E.D.
Got her off her knees,
And by the time
She's done preaching,
My math book gleams
Like gold.

23

Foreign Fare

Grandma's cooking
Shows off her Southern side:
Yams, crab cakes, mustard greens—
The kind of food I'm used to.
Then she'll go and add
Some foreigner to the bunch.
Today it's Swedish herring.
"Taste it," she says,
Passing me the plate.
The strips of fish swim raw
And silvery in pickle juices
That wrinkle my nose
With suspicion.
"Smells funny," I mumble.
"Humph!" says Grandma.
"You young folks just
Don't know what's good."
Her eyes dare me
To give the fish a try.
I sneer, on cue,
Stab a teensy scrap
And take a bite.

"Hey! This is good," I say,
Surviving the adventure.
Grandma winks at me.
"See? If you only stick
With what you know,
You miss out in life."
"Yeah, well," I shoot back,
"Looks like you got
That problem licked.
Thanks to you, my taste buds
Are gonna see the world."

Stepping Out

On Sundays
I know
Stepping out
With Grandma Mac
Means wearing my best,
So when I show up
In a nicely pressed
White dress, with
Matching shoes and purse,
A lecture is not
What I expect. Except
It's after Labor Day
And according to Grandma Mac
Wearing white is now
Officially a sin.
"Who cares?" I ask,
Wondering what Bible
She's been reading.
"*I care,*" she insists.
"White is for summer,
Not for fall."
This is not what I call
A reasonable explanation.

And it's exactly these
Fancy ideas of hers
Rubbing off on me
That give other kids
The notion
I think I'm better
Than everyone else
On the block—
Like being a kid
Around here
Isn't tough enough
Already!

Duet

One night
I steal in quiet,
Use my keys
For a change.
Catch her
Slow dancing
Across the floor,
Her eyes like
Padlocked doors,
Mournful music
From the radio
Drowning her in some
Secret memory,
And Grandma Mac
Swimming for all she
Is worth.

A soloist, plucking
The strings of his bass,
Beats back the age lines
In her face,
And suddenly
She's this young
Humming, swaying
Soft-somebody
I never knew.
But who?
I close my eyes
Let the question go
And join her
Dancing
Slow.

Grandma's Gloves

Theirs is a sweet
Place of honor:
The top dresser drawer
Where they snuggle
Next to
Fine lace pouches
Of rose sachet.
Nothing but the best
For the fabric fingers
That hug Grandma Mac's
Soft and sturdy own.
I often try them on—
The ivory cotton,
Black wool, blue suede,

Tan leather with insides
Worn and warm—
All loyal to the form
Of work-weary hands
That have spared
Mom and me
More hard times
Than we know.
I return the gloves
To their special place
With special care
And go.

• • • • • • • • • • • • • •

One evening I choked
On my chewing gum
When I caught some
Gray-haired mister
At Grandma's door
Puckering up
For her quick kisses.
I waited 'til he left,
Stared clean through him
When he passed by,
But you can bet
I gave the guy
The once-over
The second I thought
Grandma wasn't looking.
Later, when I helped her
Clear away the dishes,
She whispered in my ear,

"Don't go telling your mom
I got me a beau.
I wouldn't want her
Getting jealous."
I must've turned
Three shades of purple
On the spot,
Then laughed like crazy
To cover.
I'll say one thing, though—
I sure like the way
Grandma's mister
Made her smile.

Like Magic • • • • • • • • • • • • • • • •

To hear Grandma tell it
A toothbrush is some kind
Of magic wand.
You rub it over your teeth
Three times a day
And, *abracadabra,*
They'll last forever.
"Why you think I still got
All my teeth?" she brags.
And her teeth *do* look good,
So I suppose
She's onto something—
Except for the part
About magic.
She sure could
Use some, though.
Just last night,
When she thought
I was sleeping,
I saw her remove
Her fake hair,
Set the lifeless curls
On a wig stand,

Watched her run
A wrinkled hand
Over a scalp which, I swear,
Is growing balder
By the minute,
And I thought:
Never mind the toothbrush.
Where's a magic *hairbrush*
When you need one?

It's Christmas Eve.
Grandma and me
Huddle together outside
Of Radio City Music Hall
Bent on seeing
The Rockettes
Kick up their heels
No matter how long
We have to stand out
In the snow. Today
The sun is like some
Chilled slice of lemon,
Dripping cool light on us
While our faces freeze.
We march in place
And stamp our feet
Against the cold,
Waiting in a line
That zigzags

Down the street
And takes half an hour
To reach the ticket booth.
I would mind more
Except that Grandma
Who normally
Avoids touching
Grabs my hand
Sticks it in
The warm well
Of her coat pocket
And holds it there
What seems like
Forever.

Missing Me

When I'm gone
For more than a day,
Or am away at my dad's
For half the summer,
Grandma pretends
Not to notice.
And once I'm home,
She presses her happiness
Between pursed lips
So no smile can escape.
But who's she kidding?
The family Bible
On her nightstand,
Thick with fragile pages
That have practically
Memorized her touch,
Is the first thing
She lays hands on
When she wakes.

And the bookmark
She uses there
To hold her place
Is a photograph of me.
So I honestly
Never have to wonder
Whether Grandma Mac
Misses me
When I'm not around,
Because I know.